Fire Mask

by

Franzeska G. Ewart

Illustrated by Dylan Gibson

Jacket image based on a design by
Rebecca Morgan of Mayfield Primary School, Midlothian,
winner of the Fire Mask cover design competition.

Highly Commended entries:

Billy Adams, Lawfield Primary School, Midlothian
Cameron Chisholm, Lawfield Primary School, Midlothian
Samuel Grainger, Newtongrange Primary School, Midlothian
David Halley, Newtongrange Primary School, Midlothian
Rebecca Russell, Newtongrange Primary School, Midlothian
Holli Smith, Mayfield Primary School, Midlothian

First published in 2010 in Great Britain by
Barrington Stoke Ltd
18 Walker St, Edinburgh, EH3 7LP

www.barringtonstoke.co.uk

ISBN: 978-1-84299-762-8

Printed in Great Britain by Bell & Bain Ltd

AUTHOR ID

Name: Franzeska G. Ewart

Likes: Cats, frogs, friends, flowers, music.

Dislikes: Winter gales.

3 words that best describe me:
Imaginative, funny, sensitive.

A secret not many people know:
I often look more confident than I feel.

ILLUSTRATOR ID

Name: Dylan Gibson

Likes: Going out, walks, cycling, reading.

Dislikes: Sundays and Monday mornings!

3 words that best describe me:
Tall, talkative and hard-working.

A secret not many people know:
I hate flying!

To my friend Moira Kinniburgh

Contents

Day 1
The Story So Far ...

Hi. I'm Joshua. Josh to my friends, Squirt to my enemies.

Not that I've *got* any friends. Not any more. All I've got is Dexter.

Dexter, and this stupid diary.

Carol-Ann said I should keep the diary. Carol-Ann works at the hospital. She's a counsellor and she's supposed to be helping me with my problems.

Fat chance.

"Write down anything you like," she told me. "Your thoughts. How you're feeling. What's happening at school. At home. At the hospital. That sort of thing."

No way do I want to keep a diary. *So* not my thing. But I'm going to. Because writing's easier than talking to Carol-Ann.

Anything's easier than talking to Carol-Ann.

So, here's the story so far:

My dad was a soldier, in Iraq. He was really brave. He won a medal, and when the war was over he was going to come home, to a hero's welcome.

I couldn't wait. Neither could Mum, nor Gran, nor Larry. (My little brother Larry is also known as Larry the Demolition Man. He's six, and hell-bent on destroying our house and everything in it.)

All we wanted was to see Dad again. The "Dad" we missed like anything.

And Dad did come home. But not the way we expected. Two days before he was due to leave Iraq, he stepped on a land mine that no one knew was there.

That someone *should* have known was there.

They brought my dad home in an air ambulance, with his face burned and ripped to pieces.

He's still in the hospital. They're trying to fix his face. You can't see it though, because it's covered in a white mask. All you can see's his eyes. His blue-grey eyes.

No one knows what's going on under that mask. They've done loads of skin grafts to try to cover his burns. But they can't tell us if they'll work. No one can tell us what Dad's going to look like.

It scares me stupid, thinking about it.

It's funny, though – just writing about Dad and his mask, I've suddenly worked out that what bothers me most is the *eyes*.

They're not injured or anything. You can see they're all right. But somehow they're not Dad's eyes any more.

I've got his photo by my bed. The last photo he sent me from Iraq. He's sitting up on a tank, grinning down at the camera.

In that photo, it's not Dad's *lips* that are smiling. It's his *eyes*. They're all crinkled up at the sides, and twinkling. It looks as if *they're* laughing.

These days, though, Dad's eyes never laugh. They stare up at me, through the holes in his mask, and there's no light in them. No life.

When we go to visit Dad, I can hardly say anything to him. My mind just goes blank. It's easier not to speak, anyway. In case he notices how upset I am.

I am upset. But I'm angry too. *Raging.*

Because it shouldn't have happened. Not to my dad. Not to anyone.

"Don't bottle up your feelings, Josh," Carol-Ann keeps saying. "*Talk* about it."

That's easy enough for her to say. *She* hasn't tried talking to Mum or Gran.

Mum keeps saying she's "worried sick". She goes on and on about it, as if we don't already know. She's on tablets from the doctor, and most nights she and Gran sit in front of the TV, smoking cigarettes and drinking vodka.

And Gran knits. Terrible jumpers that I'm supposed to wear. Jumpers that don't fit, and stink of smoke.

As for Larry the Demolition Man, there's no way on God's earth I can talk to *him*. I can hardly get him to sit still long enough to force his dinner down him. All he wants to do is find things to rip, and smash, and kick, and all *I* seem to do is try and stop him.

Sometimes, mind you, I wish he'd put his foot through the TV.

There's no one at school I can talk to, either. I haven't even told Sandy, and she's my best friend.

Was my best friend.

I'm scared to tell anyone. I'm the joker, see? Squirt, the joker. Squirt, the good laugh.

If I tried to tell, I might start crying. And there is no way I'm letting anyone see me cry.

Of course, I can always talk to Dexter. Not that "Sit, boy!" and "Walkies!" is *that* great, but he always sticks his wee tongue out, and wags his wee tail, which is Dexter's way of cheering you up.

OK. That's enough for today. I'm going to bed now ...

I wouldn't admit this to Carol-Ann, but I'm feeling a bit better about keeping the diary now. Maybe it's not so bad. Maybe it helps. Makes things clearer.

Maybe that's because I'm telling my life like a story. As if it was happening to someone else.

Which is a million times better than it happening to *me*.

Day 2
If Looks Could Kill ...

I'm not sure when me and Sandy fell out.
It happened so slowly, I hardly noticed. Till
this week.

Sandy and I have always been friends,
ever since Nursery. Even our dogs are pals.
Sandy's got a spaniel called Kelsie. And even
though Kelsie's dead posh, with a pedigree
and everything, and Dexter's just a wee fat
mongrel, they get on really well. It's funny
when they go on walks together – Dexter has

to take about a hundred steps to one of Kelsie's!

I couldn't tell Sandy about Dad. I just couldn't.

I did try.

"How's your dad getting on, Josh?" she'd ask. And she'd look at me, dead close, as if she could read my thoughts.

I always think Sandy can read my thoughts ...

I'd *want* to tell her. I'd be dying to say, "I think his face has gone. Covered in scars now. Red raw, and the skin stretched too tight."

But instead, I'd end up saying, "Fine. He's fine." And then I'd turn away, make an excuse. Walk off.

Because if I stayed, I'd tell her everything. And then I'd cry. Like a baby.

I suppose that's what did it. I suppose it's my fault.

The day before yesterday, I met Sandy in the corridor at school, and she just turned away. Didn't even try to speak to me. And her eyes were sad, and hurt-looking.

The worst thing of all is, she's taken up with Tiffany. Tiffany, The Witch.

If you ask me, Tiffany's evil. I don't know why she should be, but she is.

Sandy's not bad-looking, with her nice wavy brown hair, but Tiffany's really stunning – straight blonde hair, big blue eyes, great clothes. But those eyes of hers are cold and hard. Sometimes, when she looks at you, you feel them freezing your insides.

I can't think why Sandy's taken up with Tiffany, but it seems suddenly they're joined at the hip.

Like today, when Mrs Todd told us to pick partners for the trip to the local museum. The two of them were all over one another, linking arms, and going on and on – "I'm with Sandy, Mrs Todd!" and "I'm with Tiffany, Mrs Todd!" as though they've been best buddies all their lives.

I don't trust Tiffany with Sandy. I've seen what she's done to other kids. I reckon she's got plans. Bad plans.

Today, in Art, I moved as far away from the two of them as I could. I watched them, though.

Maybe I'm paranoid, but every time I looked at them, they looked down. Then they'd nudge one another, and giggle. They're up to something. I'm sure they are.

We're making masks in Art. Mrs Todd's brought in loads to show us. My favourite is a golden cat. I like him, because his eyes are green and mysterious. Like he knows a lot of secrets.

Mrs Todd gave us white plastic masks, and showed us how to put on torn bits of paper mixed with glue. Today, the paper was dry, so we peeled it off and started to paint. I'm trying to make my own golden cat, but it's rubbish. The eyes aren't right.

"When you've cleaned your neutral masks," Mrs Todd says (because that's what you call these blank white plastic masks that have no expression at all), "put them back in the box, please."

Then she peers over her specs. "Who would like to go round with the box," she asks, "and collect the masks?"

Like a shot, Tiffany's on her feet, shouting, "Me, Mrs Todd! Can I do it, please?"

She's *begging* with Mrs Todd. She's *desperate* to be picked, like collecting masks is the coolest thing you could *ever* do.

What's *that* all about? It's only a load of old plastic masks ...

When the bell goes I head out as fast as I can, but Tiffany comes rushing round with the mask box and bangs into me. On purpose, like. She gives me one of her ice-blue looks.

There's a saying, *if looks could kill*. That was the kind of look Tiffany gave me.

And the way I feel tonight, I almost believe they *could* kill.

Day 3
White Out

I'm upset tonight. So upset, I wasn't even going to bother writing this. But then I thought I should get it down on paper. Not bottle it up.

I can't believe they did something so horrible. I hate what they did.

And I hate that they *know* ...

Last night it snowed. When I got up, the world outside was white. And, soon as I went downstairs, the shouting started.

First it was over Gran's Jumper-from-Hell.

This jumper has to be seen to be believed. It is *so* cheesy! Which is my fault, because I chose it.

"What's your favourite thing in all the world, Josh love?" Gran asked me.

"Football," I said.

So that's what she knitted. A disgusting green jumper, with a black-and-white football on the front.

The green is brighter than pea soup, and the football is all wonky round the edges. There are loads of wee holes where Gran's dropped stitches, and the left arm is a lot longer than the right.

Today, Mum wanted me to wear it to school. To make Gran happy. I told her *no way*.

Then, as we were yelling at each other, Larry came in with a mass of tangled wires and black plastic in his hand.

And the mass of tangled wires and black plastic turned out to be what was left of Mum's hair-dryer. And whose fault was it that Larry smashed it? No prizes for guessing.

That was when the second lot of shouting began.

All day at school, I felt like a big bottle, filled full with fizzy anger. All morning, and all afternoon, I kept the lid on that bottle.

I couldn't focus on my work, though. You can't, when all you want to do is explode. So I kept getting told off by Mrs Todd.

All I wanted to do was look out the window, think my angry thoughts, and keep them from bursting a hole in the top of my head. It calmed me down a bit, looking out at the snow in the playground, and the white hills beyond.

Even the sky was white. White as the sheets on Dad's hospital bed.

Somehow, I didn't *want* to stop thinking about how angry I was with Mum, or how worried I was about Dad. I just kept thinking about it. About the day they'd take the mask off.

How would I feel about Dad when his face was different?

What if his face was as blank as the snowy sky? Would we still be able to laugh together?

Would I still love him?

By home time, it was almost dark. Big flakes of snow were starting to fall.

"Don't forget we're going to the museum tomorrow," Mrs Todd said. "Wrap up warm!" Then she rushed off to dig her car out of the snow, and everyone rushed off behind her.

I was in no hurry, though. I knew the playground would be full of people shouting and yelling and pelting each other with snowballs. Today, I was in no mood for snowball fights. So I took my time packing up, then I put off the classroom light and slipped out.

In our school, all the classrooms branch off one long corridor. The corridor lights were off. No one was around.

Or so I thought.

I hurried, then. I didn't like the corridor. It was filled with grey, shadowy light, and the only sounds were my breathing and the squeak of my footsteps on the floor. I wanted out.

When I saw the first white mask floating in front of me, I thought for one moment – one mad, crazy moment – that it was Dad. I stared into the two black holes that were its eyes, and I wanted to scream. But no sound came.

I couldn't move, either. I was frozen to the spot. I stopped breathing.

In the silence, I heard *it* breathe. Then it spoke, and its voice was soft and deep.

"Hello," the mask said. "Hello, Josh, son."

I think I screamed. I reached out into the darkness below the mask, and pushed.

It had a body. A warm body.

"Josh, son!" it said again. "Not going to say hello to your old dad?"

Then it laughed. And then I knew.

I pushed again, hard. Pushed it out of my way. Pushed *her* out of my way. Her, and the stupid neutral mask she'd pinched. Then I ran.

Half-way along the corridor, a second mask appeared.

"Come to see Daddy?" it said, in the same, fake voice. "Daddy, home from the war?"

I tried to get past, but it – she – wouldn't let me. *Sandy*, my *friend*, wouldn't let me.

I turned. The first mask was there again.

Two masks danced round me. Blank, white, with black, dead eyes. And that was when I knew that Tiffany and Sandy had

24

found out about Dad. Gran must have told Sandy's gran, or something.

I tore my back-pack off. Spun it round and round and round, hard. "You stupid idiots!" I yelled. "Get out of my way!"

I wished I'd had bricks in my back-pack. I wanted to knock their stupid heads off, see their blood.

Tiffany's blood. But mostly Sandy's blood.

They ran away, then. Ran away, giggling, and shouting, "Squirt! Squirt! Daddy's little baby!" in silly voices.

I ran too. Down the corridor, past the office, and out. On the steps, I felt my legs crumble, felt myself slide and tumble and land face-down.

Lay, breathing hot, angry breath into the cold, wet snow.

I should go to sleep now. But I don't feel like sleeping. I'm all churned up inside.

Writing this hasn't made any difference, either. It hasn't made me feel any better. It's made me feel worse.

And I'm scared to sleep ...

Day 4
Bad Dream

My body hurts all over tonight, and I'm covered in cuts. My eyes just want to shut, but I really need to write this.

I need to write it, to make sense of what happened today. So that tomorrow, when I tell the police, I tell it right.

I'll start with the dream I had. The nightmare I had. Because if it hadn't been for that nightmare, maybe the whole thing wouldn't have happened.

I'm in school, walking down the dark, endless corridor. All I can see are outlines. Suddenly there's a flash, and everything's bright white.

Then Dad, in an electric wheelchair, wheels across the corridor in front of me. He's not wearing a mask, but I can't see his face. I try to shout "Dad!" but nothing comes. I run, try to follow him. But he's gone.

Then my brother Larry appears, wearing a white mask. He's got something in his hand. A picture of Dad.

"Don't!" I shout, because I know what he's going to do. But he doesn't listen.

I watch as he rips the picture into little pieces. They float to the ground like snowflakes. As I go to pick them up, I see them moving together again.

Dad's face is looking up at me, and all the rips in the paper are red, ugly scars.

Now Larry's running away, laughing. Hundreds of masks are snowing down on him. The floor's white with them. He reaches the end of the corridor, throws away his mask, and vanishes. His laughter echoes back to me.

Now Dexter's beside me, wagging his tail and barking. Wanting out. We run together, down the corridor. I hear the masks snapping and crackling beneath our feet. It's a good sound.

On we run, Dexter and me. Past the office, down the steps, out of the school.

The sky's black and filled with stars. There's a full moon. I see Dad's face in it. I think, *even the man in the moon's got scars.*

Dexter's still barking, wanting his "walkies". Suddenly I think of all the good times Dexter and Larry and me had with my dad, before he got blown up.

I wake. Anger's blinding me.

I was so angry when I woke up, I wanted to smash something. I picked up my pillow, banged it down on my bed, over and over. As if that pillow was Tiffany and Sandy.

How dare they give me such a bad nightmare? How *dare* they?

Wildly, I looked round my room for something to break, to rip, to destroy.

I remember thinking, *This is what Larry must feel like, when the anger gets too much for him.*

I pulled out my old toy box, found some plastic models, snapped off their heads.

It only made the anger worse. I looked in the box again, saw the old Hallowe'en mask, pulled it out.

I've had that mask for years. It's one of those rubbery ones, and it's pretty scary. It's got sea-blue skin, mad-looking eyes, and a mouthful of big horrible teeth.

And the hair's red and yellow, like flames swirling in a bonfire.

I stared and stared into the eyes of the mask. And the more I stared into those eyes of fire, the angrier I felt. As though the mask was sending its anger out to join my own.

Those eyes had such power! I really felt as if they could burn two holes right through my flesh and bones.

It's what fire would look like, if it was a face, I thought. *It's a Fire Mask.*

31

I put the Fire Mask on, and looked in the mirror. And that was when the brilliant idea came.

The brilliant idea that nearly killed Sandy ...

I got dressed. I put on my black top with the red skulls. I knew it would look good with the Fire Mask.

I went downstairs. When Mum saw my top, she didn't say anything. She just banged a bowl of cereal down in front of me.

I ate my breakfast. I left for school. The Fire Mask was smouldering in my pocket.

I've been to the museum hundreds of times. It's a mining museum. Dad's dad was a miner, and he used to take me.

He'd tell me stories of the old mining days, and show me all the secret places. I know that Mining Museum like the back of my hand.

When we arrived, they gave us yellow helmets. They took us to the tub circuit room, then up some steps to a metal walk-way. From the walk-way we could look down on the tubs with their loads of fake coal.

The yellow helmets had ear-phones, to tell us what everything was. I didn't listen. I wasn't interested. Today, I had only one thing on my mind.

Revenge.

"Opposite where you are standing," the voice in the ear-phones said, "you can see the control cabin. Inside are models of men at their control panels ..."

I dumped the helmet. Stared at the dusty old dummies.

I'd seen them a million times. But today, for the first time, I thought how life-like they were. As if, any minute, they could turn round and stare at you with their dark, dummy eyes.

The tub circuit room was dead noisy. There was a soundtrack playing, of metal chains clanking and men shouting, and everyone in our class was shouting too. Their feet clattered on the metal walk-ways.

Tiffany and Sandy trailed behind everyone, talking and giggling. Mrs Todd kept telling us all to be quiet.

I hung back. Let them go on. When they were far enough away, I went up to Tiffany.

"See them dummies," I said. "Sometimes they come alive."

Tiffany looked down her nose at me, and her ice-blue eyes laughed. Not the way Dad's eyes used to laugh, though. But mocking. Sneering.

"Is that a fact, Squirt?" she said, giving Sandy a look. "Is that what your daddy told you?"

"You watch," I said. "You'll see."

They doubled up with laughter. At least, Tiffany did. Sandy pretended to, but she was looking at me.

Looking at me as though she was worried about me.

When they turned and ran after the class, I didn't follow.

I know a quick way over to the other side. A narrow walk-way they don't like you using. I crossed, and crept round till I was near the cabin. I leaned over the red safety rail. Watched Mrs Todd giving out sketch pads and pencils.

37

Supposing she noticed I wasn't there?

Right under my feet, stuck to the wall, was a black metal ladder. I squeezed under the safety rail, pulled myself on.

The ladder was slippy. And it went straight down to a sort of ledge. The ledge was covered in loose stones and broken glass. Below I could see piles of rubble, with bushes and ferns growing in between. There were bits of brick-work, with rusty old pipes sticking out. And there was a great big crack in the ground.

From far, far down, I heard water dripping.

Below that big crack, I knew, was the mine shaft.

I shouldn't have climbed down that ladder. When I got to the bottom, I shouldn't have climbed over the chain with the *Danger. Keep Out* notice.

And I shouldn't have crept up the metal steps to the cabin, or pushed open the door with the *Strictly No Entry* sign.

It was anger that made me do it. Wild, seething anger, hot as the Fire Mask's flaming eyes. Hot as the fire that burned my dad's face off ...

That'll have to do. Can't write any more. Need to sleep.

I'll write the rest tomorrow ...

Day 5
Pay Back

Two police came to see me – a man and a woman. They were nicer than I expected.

I told them everything, just the way I'd written it down. All about Dad, and Tiffany and Sandy's trick, and the nightmare. I even told them about Mum being on tablets, and Gran's cheesy jumper.

All the time I was telling them, I was thinking, *they'll lock me up. They'll put me in a Young Offenders Unit.*

But the funny thing was, they weren't even angry.

Maybe they were saving their anger for someone else.

Maybe someone else should be going to a Young Offenders Unit ...

I couldn't believe that I'd actually got inside the cabin. That Mrs Todd hadn't noticed I was gone.

One good thing about being a squirt, I suppose.

I felt as if I was in a film, then. A film that turned into a horror film. This is how it went:

41

As soon as I'm in the cabin, I rip off my jacket and pull on the Fire Mask. I sit beside one of the dummy banksmen. We've got our backs to the window.

I sit as still as I can. I hear Mrs Todd shouting at everyone to put away their sketch-pads. I hear them clattering along the walk-way, louder and louder.

"Keep well back from the railing," I hear Mrs Todd saying. "Right below where we are standing, is one of the deepest mine shafts in Britain."

Everyone breathes in. Someone makes a silly noise.

"The men in the cabin controlled everything," Mrs Todd goes on. "There they are, in front of the panels."

Footsteps shuffle nearer.

"Hey, look!" someone shouts. "Three dummies!"

I'm hardly breathing now. I'm praying my plan's going to work.

The footsteps start to move away. I freeze. Will Tiffany and Sandy follow?

I hear Sandy's voice.

"D'you think that was true, what Josh said?"

"*Squirt*," Tiffany answers, and her voice is really angry. "What *Squirt* said. Of course it wasn't true. Don't be stupid."

I don't waste a second. I jump to my feet, throw myself towards them. And I make the biggest, scariest sound I can. The roaring sound of fire.

Fire searing through hair, burning it off. Fire, charring skin and destroying smiles. Fire, wrecking lives forever.

I stick my blue rubber face hard against the glass, and I keep on roaring. I claw at the glass with my fingers. I boot the glass with my feet.

And, you know, I really *feel* like fire. Like every bit of anger is exploding out into great furious red flames.

It's the best feeling in the world.

After about five seconds, of course, Tiffany and Sandy work out what's happening. But before they do, they nearly die of fright! Their faces are like masks of sheer horror.

When they see it's just me, they look at one another. Then they stand, mouths open, staring. Livid.

I don't know what I expected them to do next, but it sure as hell wasn't what they *did* do.

"Get the Squirt!" shouts Tiffany. "Kill the Squirt!" and she pushes Sandy up against the safety rail.

Pushes her up, so she's leaning right over.

I've taken the Fire Mask off, and I'm through the cabin door and down the steps, shouting at Tiffany to stop. No way should Sandy be on that rail. No way.

I'm on the ledge, starting to climb up the black metal ladder. I'm not believing what Tiffany's saying.

"Get over that rail," she's telling Sandy. "Don't let him up! Stand on his hands, the stupid useless Squirt!"

Then I see her push Sandy right up, so she's rocking back and forth on her tummy on the top rail.

"Turn a somersault!" Tiffany's shouting. "Get over!"

Sandy's our school gymnastic champion. She can do just about anything.

But a somersault over a rail, metres away from the deepest mine shaft in Britain?

I'm half-way up the ladder, yelling at her. "Go back, Sandy!" but I can see she isn't going back.

She doesn't *dare* go back. If Tiffany says "*get over*", you get over.

She curls tight, does a somersault, and then she's on the narrow ledge beside the cage. Her foot's level with one of my hands.

"Go *on*!" Tiffany's yelling. "Break his fingers!"

I look up at Sandy, and Sandy looks down at me. Her eyes are bright with tears. "Sorry, Josh," she whispers.

My eyes are wet too, and all of a sudden I don't care who sees. Because I'm sorry too. Sorry that I didn't trust myself to tell her all about my dad. Sorry that I drove her away.

"Get on that ladder!" Tiffany's shouting. "Get him!"

Sandy still doesn't move. And when Tiffany speaks again, she's not shouting any more. Her voice is low. She's asking a question. A terrible question.

"Ever seen an animal die from poison, Sandy? Ever seen a *dog* die from poison?"

A noise like a sob comes from Sandy's throat. She takes a step down the ladder. Then another. Then another.

Then the film changes to slow motion. And I know that life will never be the same again ...

Tomorrow's the last day I write this diary. Because, you know what? I'm not going to need it any more.

I've got another plan, you see. Another brilliant plan.

But, this one *is* brilliant.

Day 6
The Brilliant Plan

I've never felt so good as I do tonight.
Never, since Dad's accident.

Normally, when I come back from visiting
Dad, I'm all churned up. But not tonight.

Tonight, I talked to Dad. Told him
everything.

Everything.

How Sandy fell, slipped on the metal ladder, tumbled down onto the ledge. Lost her footing on a pile of loose stones.

Rolled over and over the rubble. Landed on the far side of the big crack.

Face down, with her feet hanging over the mine shaft.

How I crawled over the rubble till I got to the crack.

How scared I felt. How desperate.

The crack was far too wide to step across. There were old wooden planks lying across part of it. The only way to reach Sandy was to crawl across that rotten wood.

I called to Sandy, told her to pull herself away from the mine shaft. But she didn't move. Didn't speak.

That was when I thought she was dead.

That was when I thought I'd killed her.

I lay down flat, edged my way out, got near enough to see.

Her face was purple. There was a gurgling sound coming from the back of her throat. Then, she spoke. "My neck ..." she said.

And then I saw why she couldn't move.

Sandy wears a golden "S" round her neck. It's actually a dollar sign, but she thinks it's an "S" for "Sandy". It's on a long gold chain, and that chain had got hooked round a twisted mass of piping.

It was tight round her neck. Choking her.

I knew she couldn't last long like that. And the rubble she was lying on was slowly sliding downwards. Pulling her downwards.

Down towards the mine shaft. Pulling the chain tighter and tighter.

I hoped Tiffany had gone for help. But I couldn't wait. I had to get to Sandy *now*.

I edged further over the crack. "It's OK," I told her. "You're going to be fine."

Then I felt the wood heave below me. There was a creaking sound, and bits fell off. Ages later, I heard them splash into the water below.

I froze with fear then. I just lay, watching Sandy's face turn deeper and deeper purple. Watching her life drain away.

That was when I heard Dad's voice.

From somewhere far, far away, it came. From a different life. Saying what he always used to say, when I was worried or scared about something.

"If you think you can do it, Josh," he'd always tell me, "you can do it."

And suddenly, the memory of Dad's words made me feel strong. I thought of all the things he'd had to do in the war. I thought how brave he was.

How brave he *is*, lying day after day in that hospital. Hidden behind a mask that's soon got to come off.

There was a clump of ferns, just beside Sandy. They had strong stems. Strong enough to hold me – maybe. I threw myself forwards, crashed down on the rotten wood. Prayed I wouldn't crash through.

I missed.

I did the same again. This time, the wood below me splintered and gave way. There was nothing beneath me. Just space. But I had hold of the fern stems.

I pulled myself over, grabbed a piece of pipe, hauled at it. For a moment both my feet dangled down. I felt my body slip downwards. My arms were nearly ripped out of their sockets, but somehow I kept hold of the pipe. Dragged myself out.

Took hold of the gold chain. Hauled at it till it snapped. Put both arms under Sandy's and pulled her clear of the mine shaft.

Held her. Told her she'd be all right now. Waited till the miners came, and lifted us, and held us safe in their strong old arms.

That was what I told Dad tonight. How, suddenly, I'd felt strong.

How his words had made me feel strong.

But before I told him, I did my brilliant plan. The brilliant plan that *was* brilliant. And simple, too.

I just put on a mask.

Not a real mask, though. Not this time.
I put on an invisible mask.

I pulled my face into a silly big smile. I
became Squirt the Joker again.

Well ... Josh the Joker, actually.

And I wore Gran's cheesy jumper, and
when I got to Dad's bed, I stood, grinning like
an idiot, flapping the long sleeve at him.

"Like the latest fashion?" I said. And I
laughed.

I didn't feel one bit like laughing. But I
laughed.

And you know what? I saw Dad's eyes
laugh too. Then he patted the bed and I sat
beside him, close. Bent over the mask. Looked

into his blue-grey, laughing eyes, and listened.

"Hear you've been in the wars, Josh," he said. "You all right?"

I nodded.

"Yes," I said. "I'm all right. So is Sandy."

Then I told him everything. And it was good to talk to him again, after so long.

When I'd finished, we just sat. For ages. And you know what? All the life was back in his eyes. It felt like old times, before the accident. Dad and me, and nothing we couldn't say.

Soon, they'll take Dad's mask off. It's not going to be easy for any of us, but maybe it'll be better than not knowing.

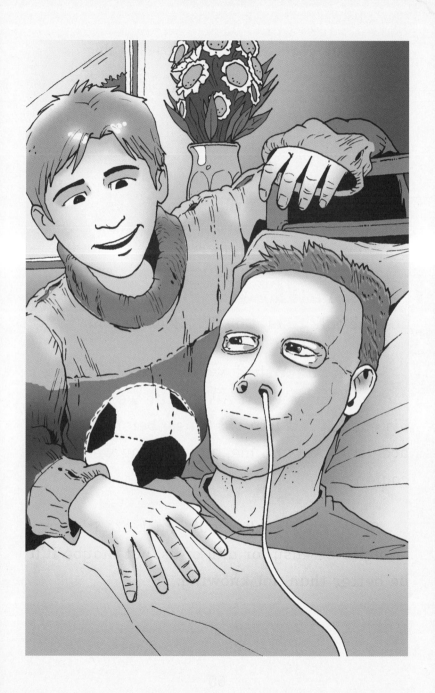

Things are better anyway, now I've got Sandy back. Now I know I can talk to her about *anything*. Now I'm not scared of letting her see me cry.

And whatever Dad looks like, at least I know his eyes can still laugh. So, whatever's below that mask, we'll face it. Together.

This book was written in collaboration with pupils from six primary schools in Midlothian.

With special thanks to:

Gorebridge Primary School P5/6

In particular – William Aitken, Chloe Cocking, Chloe Cooper, Keiran Donald, Calum Fowler, Lucy Galbraith, Sarah Hiddleston, Abigail Miller, Craig Reid, Eleanor Scott, Mikey Sneddon, Aidan Walters

Lawfield Primary School P5

In particular – Cameron Chisholm, Kyle Maben, Hamish Murphy, Ryan Paterson, Rachel Paul, Danniella Rowley, Lewis Sutherland, Kayleigh Williamson

Mayfield Primary School P7

In particular – Iona Balfour, Rachel Devine, Cody Ferguson, Dylan Jack, Thomas Kidd, Kaitlyn Morgan, Jemma Pottinger, Dale Severn

Moorfoot Primary School P6/7

In particular – Ewan Bruce, Moray Cresswell, Kirsten Dryburgh, Raakshaana Gnanamurali, Olivia Gooch, Eilidh Hudson, Eilidh Lawrie, Steven Lennie, Afton Street, Paul Wilson, Samantha Wilson

Newtongrange Primary School P7B

In particular – Catherine Allan, Jamie Allison, Jordan Cunningham, Nathan Gough, David Halley, Calum McEwan, Samantha Telfer, Jack Webster, Alyssa Wilson

Stobhill Primary School P5/6

In particular – Andrew Guild, Georgia Lawrence, Kieran Merrilees, Lauren Miller, Lisa Robertson, Keiran Wagley

With special thanks to those who commented
on the text before publication:

Sean Bett
Kathy Butcher
Bryn Davis
Allyse Hill
Sam Hollidge
Rebecca Mann
Hollie Parsons
Deborah Rosen
Edward Rosen
Leanne Taylor
Craig Telford
Jayne Walker-Harris